ONE SNOWY AMISH NIGHT

NAOMI ZOOK

FOREWORD

PROLOGUE

$\mathcal{I}$t was the faint, tinny sound of canned sitcom laughter blasting through the paper-thin walls of their apartment that woke nine-year-old Ripley.

She blinked several times, squinting as she lay cocooned in the warm bed. Gecko's head rested on her shoulder, the battered action man figure that he'd squabbled over with Axel earlier still clutched in his small fist. Judd's foot was wedged painfully against her back. She carefully extricated herself from the tangle of her siblings' limbs, mindful not to wake them.

The sporadic glow of the neighbors' Christmas lights flashed through the broken, slatted blinds, illuminating her path across the toy-littered floor. Marvel action figures lay alongside a capeless Superman. The decapitated remains of an old Barbie doll now wore Superman's cape.

All were casualties of living with four brothers in a tiny apartment with no room of her own.

She opened the living room door, and a sigh escaped her. Her mother was sprawled on the sofa, passed out, her arm dangling over the edge toward where an empty bottle of liquor lay discarded on its side. Her face was slack with slumber, the red and green flickers that reached through the curtainless windows giving her a garish, macabre appearance.

On the other side of the sofa, Ripley's oldest brother Ferris sat with his long legs tucked under him. The dim glow of the old TV flickered across his features as he stared blankly at the screen. The laughter from the sitcom audience rattled the room once again.

"Turn it down," Ripley hissed, being careful not to wake their mom.

They were all named after '80s movie characters, a quirk of their mother's eclectic movie tastes. Ferris, true to his namesake, embraced his rebellious streak and ignored her entirely.

Tinsel hooked around various pieces of

furniture in the room danced in the light from the TV. Ripley noticed the half-wrapped gifts littering the table. "What's all this?" she gestured towards the clutter.

Ferris' dark eyes, identical to hers, flicked to the scattering of gold paper and half-wrapped boxes that had been abandoned. "Mind your own beeswax," he muttered. "You should be in bed, Rip."

"But the TV's too loud," she insisted, folding her arms over her thin nightshirt.

Ferris didn't move, his eyes fixated on the TV screen once more.

Ripley growled in frustration. "Ferris! Turn it down! You don't want to wake up Mom."

Ferris snorted at her then, and Ripley knew it was because not even an exploding device detonated in the middle of the living room would wake their Mom from one of her drunken stupors.

For a moment, her attention was snagged by the characters playing out a scene on the TV until a shiver reminded her that the furnace had run out of fuel two days ago. Her Mom had lost yet another job, and there was no money to refill the tank.

"Mum was trying to wrap those, wasn't

she?" Ripley guessed, her curious gaze going back to the table.

Ferris grunted at her.

Christmases had never been normal in their household, not even before Dad had run off with the neighbor's daughter, taking the car and their mom's stash of cash from the Star Wars cookie jar.

Last year, there hadn't been any presents under the tree. At least this year, Mom had managed to scrape together enough money together to buy them some gifts. Remembering Gecko and Judd's little faces when there hadn't been anything for them to unwrap on Christmas morning, Ripley decided to finish what her mom had started.

She walked to the table and ran an assessing gaze over it, trying to figure out which box belonged to which sibling. Amidst the usual chaos of discarded overdue bills and empty coffee cups, she picked up the box that had evidently been abandoned halfway through and began to awkwardly fold the paper. She struggled with the Scotch tape; all the while acutely aware of her brother's watchful gaze.

After a few moments, a soft blanket settled over her shoulders, followed by the TV volume going down. Finally, Ferris sat next to her at the table. He watched her as she clumsily folded the paper, struggling to hold it in place and pull off the tape at the same time.

"It's like watching a monkey try to play Tetris," he said as he took the box from her. He handed her the roll of tape. "Pull me some pieces off that." Working swiftly, he smoothed the edges and tucked the corners, his movements deft and surer than hers.

They folded, stuck. Folded, stuck.

She caught her brother's eye and offered him a small, grateful smile. A truce was forged in the quiet hours of the night.

"I don't wanna hear it," Ferris muttered quietly, rolling his eyes.

"Wasn't gonna say anything," she grinned. Ferris could be the biggest pain in her butt, and most days, she could happily throttle him. But her big brother had a softer side.

They worked quietly side-by-side, finishing wrapping the gifts so that their siblings would have a better Christmas.

And Ripley made herself a promise that someday, when she had children of her own, her life would be different from this.

Her children wouldn't have to wonder

5

whether or not their dad would take off and then pretend that his children didn't exist. She wouldn't spend her hard-earned money on drink to 'take the edge off' a bad day, when her kids were hungry. They wouldn't have to worry about whether or not the rent would be paid.

And her children would never, ever have to wrap their own Christmas presents.

RIPLEY

"*N*o! No! No!" Nathan Campbell grumbled, banging a fist on the steering wheel. "Dang it!"

Ripley frowned, blinking blearily around the darkened interior of the car. "Nate?" She murmured sleepily when she took in her husband's frustrated profile. "What's wrong?"

"Sorry, honey, I didn't mean to wake you."

"I was just resting my eyes," she joked, throwing back his usual response whenever she caught him napping on the sofa.

He didn't smile. "The car won't start," his voice was strained.

Her dark eyes widened like saucers. "What? You just had it serviced."

"I know," he gritted out. Her usually unflappable giant of a husband turned to look at her. The lights from the dashboard illuminated the sharp planes of his face. "It just... died. Rolled to a stop."

As though to illustrate his point, he turned the engine. It spluttered, making a clunking metallic sound, but didn't catch. It coughed repeatedly then died. "Stupid piece of–"

"*Nathan!*" Ripley chided him. She stared at her husband, who was gripping the steering wheel as if he wanted to yank it off.

"Sorry," he muttered, "but this is hardly ideal, Rip."

Ripley placed her hand across her protruding stomach and looked out of the window. Darkness had fallen. Beyond the vehicle, snow swirled, turning the world into a frozen realm. She could barely see anything through the falling snow. "Where...where are we?"

"Somewhere between home and Cleveland," he told her, holding up his cell phone closer to the windshield and moved it about. His glasses reflected the screen's glow. "Do you have any cell reception?

"Let me check." Ripley took her time adjusting the seat that she'd inclined to take a nap in, her bulky tummy meaning that she struggled to reach for her purse.

She pulled out her cell, though the screen remained black. "Mine is dead," she inserted regretfully. "I forgot to charge it before we left."

"Babe…" His green eyes conveyed a world of meaning in that one word. He'd repeatedly banged on at her about the importance of her keeping her phone charged, especially now that she was in her last trimester.

"You're with me, so I relaxed a little," she reasoned, trying to keep her tone even. It wouldn't do either of them any good to argue right now.

"All right," he sighed. "Hold on. Let me see if I can get some reception outside."

Before she could protest at being left alone, Nate opened the car door and slipped out. She reached for her phone, pressing the power button several times in the vain hope there was still some juice left in the battery. But even if it did, who would she call? She wouldn't want to worry her family. And what mechanic would come out in such terrible weather? The phone remained dark.

Her thoughts echoed Nate's curse word.

She jerked a little when Nate opened the door

and slid back into the car. Flecks of snow had gathered on his black hair and brows, making him look like an old man. In another situation, she would have found it funny and teased him about it, but now she was starting to freak out.

No cell reception, a broken vehicle and a blizzard. It sounded like one of those disaster movies that Axel always made her watch.

"I'm sorry. I didn't mean to startle you. I couldn't get even a bar," he informed her with a deep sigh.

"Do you know where we are?" she asked in a small voice as she tried to hide her unease from her husband.

Nate looked up from his phone, his dark brows meeting as he searched her face. From the moment they'd met, Nate had been dependable. After a lifetime of being let down, she'd taken a while to begin to trust him. He reached across the console to take her hand.

"Please don't be scared, honey. I'll find a way to get us out of here," he uttered in a soft voice.

"But how? We're in the middle of nowhere," she pointed out, even though she didn't like being a naysayer.

He offered her a small smile. "Have I ever let you down?"

She shook her head, but she couldn't return his smile.

Regret filled her. She hadn't wanted to come. Nate had been the one to push her into spending Christmas with her mom. After all these years and with her mom's recent diagnosis, he'd guilted her into making the trip when he'd pointed out that they might not have many more Christmas's left with her mom in this world.

Of course, Nate Campbell's childhood had been vastly different to hers. To him, Christmas was a magical time filled with laughter, love and happiness. It was why she'd much preferred spending Christmas with his parents.

Saying *I told you so* now wouldn't help either of them.

"I'm sorry," he whispered, his hand resting briefly on her rounded stomach.

She threaded her fingers through his hair and gave his dark mop a tug, turning his head to give her husband a kiss. "You thought you were doing the right thing by putting the car in the garage. These things are sent to test us, right?"

Nate caught her face between his palms. "Ripley Campbell, that sounds almost spiritual."

She rolled her eyes at him. "You must have brain freeze. You know I don't believe in any of that stuff anymore."

His teeth flashed white and even in a grin. "Don't you let my mom hear you say that."

Deanna Campbell would be horrified to know that her daughter-in-law no longer believed in the Lord. Nate's mom attended church and went above and beyond for those less fortunate than she in their small town.

"You won't breathe a word to your mother," Ripley told him, "else I'll tell her that you prefer my cinnamon bakes."

"You don't play fair," he said.

Ripley shrugged. "Growing up with four brothers makes you mean," she gave him a shove. "Now get off me, you're pushing the baby into my bladder."

He sat up immediately with an apology. "We should have been in Cleveland by now." He sighed. "We would have been if Wilson had allowed me to take the holiday leave I requested."

Nate's boss was a bit of a tyrant. More than once, Ripley had wanted to go down to the office, chock full of stuffy accountants, and give Bob Wilson a piece of her mind. Nate deserved better than his rotten boss.

Nate clicked his tongue. "It's times like this that I wish I was like Ferris."

"Honey," Ripley curved a hand around his head, "You're not a royal pain in my butt."

Nate shot her a deadpan look. "I meant being good with cars like he is. I'm hopeless with them. I wouldn't know where to start with that maze of pipes and wires."

"What are we going to do?"

"Hold on," he opened the door and quickly shut it, but not before an icy blast of air slid over her. His form was quickly swallowed in the haze, leaving her alone in the silence. She reached in the back of the car and tugged her coat free, laying it across her body like a blanket.

All those years of watching scary movies forced a kaleidoscope of horror-filled scenarios to spin through her head. She lay her hands across her abdomen protectively.

Nate slid back in the car once again, blowing hard. "Good grief, it's freezing," he blew into his hands. "Right, we're in a small town. Farming community. I'd say Amish, judging by some of the signs I can see along the side of the road."

She turned to gawk at him. "Amish?" Her forehead wrinkled as she tried to remember what she knew about the Amish. Not much, she concluded, other than they dressed funny. "Aren't they the ones who wear only black and white clothes, hats, suspenders, and stuff like that?" she questioned.

He chuckled. "I don't think they'd appreciate being described like that."

She turned to look out the window, adjusting herself. "Erm... honey, I know this is the wrong time to bring this up, but I need to use the bathroom ASAP."

He looked at her with sheer panic in his green eyes. "What?"

She looked at him apologetically, understanding how frustrated he felt at that moment. "I'm sorry, but you know I can't hold it."

He nodded and gazed out of the window. "Okay. I can't see anything like a motel in the vicinity. I wonder if someone will let you use their bathroom."

Her face reddened a little. She really hated to ask for help from people she didn't know. Besides, she didn't know the kind of reception they would get if they went to ask for help. Maybe she could hold it.

The tiny foot stretching against her abdomen wall put paid to that notion.

"Nate, I don't want to disturb anyone, particularly people I know little about, but I really need to use the bathroom."

"Right." Nate angled his head trying to see through the fogged-up windshield. "I only saw one house with lights from the road. I'll go and knock on their door and ask for permission for you to use their bathroom."

She undid her seatbelt. "I'll go with you."

"No, please. I don't want you out in such weather if I'm turned away."

"I can't stay here without you," she said quickly, fear edging her voice. "What if something happens to you?"

"This isn't the movies, Rip," he smiled. "The worst they can do is tell me no. Nothing else is gonna happen, babe."

"I wish I had your confidence, but I'll worry

myself silly until you come back. Look at it this way. If I come with you, you won't have to come back for me."

"Okay," he said in a resigned tone. "Like always, you make a convincing argument."

Her oval face softened in a genuine smile. She followed his fuzzy form as he got out of the car, his head ducked against the fat snowflakes. He walked around the hood to open her door.

The icy blast hit her as soon as she got out. She wrestled with her coat, tugging up the hood over her dark curls as Nate fastened it for her.

"Come on!" He slipped his hand in hers and guided her across the road.

It was slow going. The asphalt was buried under a heavy blanket of snow. She had to squint her eyes against the flurries, the snow creaking and crunching under her winter boots. She held on tight to Nate, terrified that she might slip.

Perhaps she should have stayed behind in the car. She almost regretted insisting on going with her husband. The warmth of the car was sure better than the icy weather. The snow concealed bumps and dips. Trip hazards everywhere.

If anything to her happened now...

She shoved the real fear back. She was in her final trimester. She held onto the hope that this time, everything would be fine.

A small house loomed at the end of the long drive they were walking along. Eyes narrowed against the whiteout; she could just about make out lights. Not bright, harsh white lights. Gentle, yellowy-orange glows of candles, shining softly in the windows.

Candles in a snowstorm could only mean one thing. The snowstorm had knocked the power out.

Nate knocked on the door three times. "Are you okay?"

She could only nod, her breathing heavy. Her heart raced nauseously. She heard the muted thud of footsteps approaching and then wondered what kind of reception waited for them on the other side of the door.

SADIE

"*D*anke for that delicious meal," Henry Weaver told his wife as she cleared the table.

"Thank you, too, for eating and cleaning the plate. I won't have to use much soap to wash it," Sadie Weaver teased her husband.

Grinning and rubbing his brown beard, Henry remarked, "It's the least I could do to make work easier for you."

Laughing softly, Sadie took the plates to the kitchen, where she quickly did the few dishes before she joined her husband in the sitting room for a cup of *kaffe*.

Henry had his long legs stretched out in front of him, his boots propped on a small footrest he'd

made for their home. He'd crafted almost everything in this room by hand, working long after
his working day as a cabinetmaker had finished
to build a home for her. He regarded her sleepily.

"Danke, Liebchen."

A fire roared in the hearth. The modest
sitting room had been decorated ready for
Christmas in two days time when his family
would be joining them. Winter was Henry's
favorite season, and he enjoyed the Christmas
celebrations. Her family stayed home for
Christmas and hosted a big party on New
Year's day instead. She hadn't been in the mood
this year, so Henry had been the one to deco-
rate their home.

Baskets filled the windows, crammed full of
evergreen branches. Simple paper stars and
hand-tied ribbons completed the pretty
display. Along the oak mantlepiece, he'd stuck
sprigs of holly into the garland of pine and
cedar. The natural foliage scented the air with
fresh, crisp scents of the outside, and fitted
harmoniously with her handmade candles that
burned around the room.

Her niece had made strings made of
popcorn and Henry had included them in his

cheerful presentation as a touch of whimsy and a reminder of the season's joys.

She sat on the sofa. Her gaze roamed around the warm room with detachment. She wanted to put away the rest of the adornments – the handmade Christmas cards from the neighbors, the wreath with its shiny red berries popping against the dark green foliage, and the colorful mini quilts.

She wanted to put it all away and just try to move on.

She was in no mood for celebrating with friends. She didn't want to see all the family, or have to laugh and smile, and pretend that everything was alright in her world.

This Christmas was meant to be so very different...

"The snow is coming down again," Henry indicated the window as he took a sip from his cup of coffee. "I hope that it won't stop people coming by for Christmas."

Sadie shrugged. "I wouldn't mind if we spent the day alone."

His round face contorted in a frown. "You love Christmas."

She forced herself to smile. She loved him so much; she didn't want to say anything that would make him unhappy. Only *Gott* truly understood how she felt. He'd been so busy with work, trying to get all of the furniture orders ready for his customers, it seemed like his feet hadn't touched the ground. She'd hardly seen him, what with all the extra work he'd been doing. He probably hadn't noticed the melancholy that shrouded her like a cloak.

He's doing it for you, for your lives together, a small voice reminded her.

She bowed her head and stared into her cup to avoid answering. How could she explain things to him in a way that he would understand what she was going through?

"Sadie?" Henry prompted. The gentle tone brought tears to her eyes.

She willed them back. Forced herself to look at him. "I'm okay."

Henry drew closer to his wife on the sofa. "You are my *fraa*," he explained quietly, embracing her. "You don't have to pretend everything is okay with me. I know it isn't."

Gratitude filled her as she stared into his brown eyes. This was one of the reasons she'd agreed to become his wife.

"*Gott* has a plan, *jah?*"

His words – meant to reassure – pushed a

spear of ugly emotion through her. It might be in His plan. Losing a child still hurt.

Before she could answer, they heard a knock on the door. They looked towards the door and then at each other.

"Are you expecting anyone?" Henry questioned her.

"*Nee.*"

They were at the edge of town, far enough away that it discouraged door-to-door sales, or anything of that nature.

"What kind of crazy person would be out in this?" Henry gestured at the snow that filled the window ledge.

"Maybe one of your *narrish* customers, wondering why you haven't finished their table yet?" Sadie quipped.

Chortling, he tapped her nose.

He nudged the footstool out of the way with his foot and stood up. Curious, she followed her husband. Henry lit their way with an oil lamp, the soft glow dancing on the walls. He set it down on the sideboard near the front door. Her eyes widened when Henry opened the door, and she saw two *Englischers* standing there in thick coats.

"Good evening. I'm sorry for disturbing

your evening. Our car broke down over there," the man extended a gloved finger back towards the road. "Yours was the only house we could see that had lights on." He was tall, taller than Henry, with broad shoulders and big hands. He had a warm smile, kind eyes that shone behind his glasses. "We have a... peculiar request. My wife needs to use the... restroom. I don't know if you'd be kind enough to allow her to ease herself," he implored.

Henry and Sadie shared a look of utter amazement. *Englischers* passed through their small town all the time, but none of them had ever stopped to ask for help. Sadie couldn't understand what they would be doing out in this weather and at this time of the day.

"Please," Sadie heard the woman say in a sweet voice, and she shook herself from her motionless state.

"*Jah.* Of course, please come in," Sadie invited. "I'll show you where it is."

The couple sighed with relief, and the man helped his wife forward as Henry and Sadie moved away from the door. Sadie's brown eyes widened a little when she saw the woman's protruding stomach against her heavy coat.

Sadie tamped down on the white-hot stab of jealousy that lanced through her.

"Oh, thank you," the woman exclaimed. "It's freezing out there. There's no way I could have...gone out there."

Sadie's smile was brittle as emotions flooded her. "I understand," she picked up the lamp from the sideboard, and led the waddling woman through their humble home towards the back.

"This weather is something, huh," the woman exclaimed. "How long has the power been out?"

Sadie frowned over her shoulder at the woman. "We don't use electricity."

The woman looked startled. "Oh, I'm so sorry, forgive my ignorance. I assumed that because you had the lamp in your hand..."

Sadie stopped in front of the bathroom door, a small smile on her face as she waved the apology. "Here you are. We have an automatic solar powered light in there. Ours is a progressive community, else you'd be taking the lamp in there with you."

The woman stared at her for a moment, uncertain. "No power at all? How do you watch TV?"

Sadie's lips flickered with laughter at the horror creasing her face. "I've only ever seen a television once, when I visited New York with my *schwester* – my sister," she clarified. "I watched an episode of something called *Friends*. I liked it."

The woman blinked at her. "You've never seen a movie?"

Sadie shook her head, then said, "Did you need to go in there?"

"Yes! Yes, I do."

Sadie decided to wait by the door for her in case she needed help. She was used to the stares by the *Englischers* as they passed through the town. Cars would slow down – mostly – when she was in the buggy, and she'd learned to ignore them. But the abject horror in which the newcomer had looked at her was more amusing than upsetting.

The sounds of the woman using the facilities carried, and she could also hear the rumble of the masculine voices down the corridor. Being stranded was scary, but stranded in a blizzard and pregnant?

A feeling of longing struck her, but she quickly pushed it away.

Focus on helping her and not your own troubles, she told herself inwardly.

Just then, the bathroom door opened, and the woman stepped out of it, looking flushed, her coat laid over her arm. Startled, she looked up at Sadie.

"Sorry," Sadie's mouth bent. "I didn't mean to scare you. I didn't want you to have to walk back in the dark."

"That's kind," the woman rubbed her belly. "I can't tell you how much better I feel. Things get quite desperate at this stage."

Sadie made herself smile. "How far along are you?"

"Nearly there," she patted her stomach in a way that made envy pool in her stomach. "My due date is next month."

Sadie firmed her mouth, her throat working to hold back that hot tears that wanted to spring forth.

"Honey? Everything alright?"

"Much better," the *Englischer* called back to her husband. "He's a worrier," she added softly, though there was no malice in her face. "This is our first child."

Pain quivered in her throat and Sadie bit her lip to quell the tears. In the silence, the other woman's brow furrowed. The warm light lit up her pretty features. Wild dark curls framed her face. The nose piercing glinted, and Sadie could see the edge of what looked like a bird's wing tattoo where the sleeve of her t-shirt ended.

"Ma'am, are you… okay? Have–have I upset you?"

Sadie could only shake her head as she tried to get herself under control. "Forgive me," she said huskily, embarrassment staining her face as she swallowed several times.

"Nothing to forgive," the woman said. "My name is Ripley."

Good, that was good, Sadie nodded. Mundane chitchat. Something normal to focus on. She exhaled slowly. "My name is Sadie. I haven't heard such a name before. What does it mean?"

The woman wrinkled her nose. "Oh, please don't get me started. I hate the name."

"But why? Your parents chose the name for you. It's a blessing."

The woman chuckled. "My mom is a huge fan of the 80's films. I was named after the Alien one. You know the Alien movie with Sigourney Weaver?"

Sadie shook her head. "No movies, remember?"

They began to walk back down the corridor. "Oh," Ripley said, "then you won't fully understand the complete cringe-fest of my childhood. I have four brothers, you see?"

"Four?"

"Yup. Ferris, Axel, Gecko, all film character names from her favorites. Plus, mom had an unhealthy lust for an actor named Judd Nelson, and that's what she named my youngest brother. It could be worse," she chuckled, "I was in school with a guy named Brownie."

Although some of her friends had left home and traveled afar for their *Rumspringa*, Sadie had been perfectly content to stay at home. She hadn't seen the need to explore because she knew that she wanted to accept the Amish lifestyle. Until now, she'd never questioned her decision, but now she found herself wondering what else she'd not known about the *Englischer's* world.

HENRY

*H*enry smiled awkwardly at the giant of a man standing in his sitting room. In his line of work, he often dealt with customers from the *Englischer* world who were seeking high quality, handmade furniture. Still, none of them had ever stood in his humble sitting room, staring around the place as if they'd stepped into a brand-new world.

Henry followed the stranger's eyes around the space and wondered how very different their home was.

"Thank you for this," the stranger offered him a nervous smile, which settled henry somewhat.

"It's not a problem," Henry shrugged, and searched for something to say in the silence that stretched between them. He heard the murmur of female voices fade away and longed for Sadie's ability to be able to find conversation in the most unusual of places.

"I'm Nathan, Nathan Campbell," the man stuck out his hand. "Everyone calls me Nate, though."

"Henry Weaver. It's a pleasure meeting you. Pardon me for asking, but what are you doing out in such terrible weather? It has been snowing nonstop for days."

Nate sighed heavily. "I didn't think to check the weather report before we left. It was all very last minute. We're going to Cleveland to see Ripley – that's my wife, Ripley," Nate motioned at the door, "we're going to see her mom. We weren't going to go. She... it's difficult to explain – not that you're asking for an explanation," Nate stuck his hands deep in his jeans. He exhaled again, shook his head as if trying to steady himself. "Sorry. The car breaking down has thrown me for a loop. I had it serviced two days ago especially for the trip. Work made it impossible for me to get away sooner and finalize everything."

Henry felt for the other *mann*. He was

clearly frazzled, running his hands through his hair.

His sharp green eyes looked up. "I'm sorry to ask for more help when you've already let us in to your home, but would you have a phone I could use? I need to call for a rescue. I have no cell reception and Rip's baby brain means that she forgot to charge hers."

"*Ach*, no," Henry shook his head. "We don't have modern appliances in our homes."

Nate slapped a hand to his head. "Of course, sorry, I didn't think."

More fidgeting.

"The bishop is the only one who has a home phone for emergencies."

The green eyes lit up. "Fantastic. Would he let me use it?"

"For sure and certain," Henry nodded, "he's across the town though. It's a perilous walk in this weather."

"That's okay," Nate waved. "If you can give me some directions, that would be wonderful."

Henry grimaced. The hour was late, and, in this weather, it would take another hour to get to the Bishop's *haus* on foot.

He heard the women chatting as they walked back down the hallway and looked up.

One look at the astonishment on Sadie's face drew his brows together. But beneath that, he noticed her overly bright eyes.

A fragility to her that hadn't been there until a few months ago.

All too often these days, he'd walk into a room, and she'd jerk herself out of her reverie. She'd claim that she was fine.

She was far from it.

He wished that he could take the burden from her shoulders. Bishop Schneider had counselled him, advising him to give her time and space. Henry was used to fixing things for others, for making people smile.

This was something that he couldn't fix.

And he knew that she was struggling over the heavily pregnant woman who followed behind her.

"Better?" Nate crossed to his wife, touching her as if reassuring himself.

The wife nodded. "Much."

"Henry, this is Ripley," he introduced her. "Henry here was just telling me that the Bishop has a phone we can use to call a rescue. It's across town."

Ripley looked a little relieved, her dark eyes

moving between Sadie and Henry. "That's good news."

Henry reached for Sadie's hand, squeezing it reassuringly.

"Did you forget the Bishop has gone to see his son?"

Henry glanced down at Sadie. "Of course, you're right!"

"So...no phone?" Nate's nervous shifting was back.

"Someone will have it," Henry tried to reassure him. "The Bishop wouldn't leave the *Ordnung* without means of contact. One of the other elders will have it. But..." Henry hesitated before replying. "Well, it's getting late now. Many people are early risers, so they take to bed early. Especially in the winter. I... I don't think it's a good idea to be knocking on all doors."

"You're right," Nate settled an arm around Ripley. They exchanged a look that conveyed their worries. "Well, we'll think of something. Thanks again for letting her use your toilet. Come on, honey."

The couple turned for the door. Sadie's hand tightened on his and she frowned up at him.

He quirked a dark brow at her. "What?" He mouthed.

Sadie's eyes moved between the retreating couple and back again. He caught her sigh. "Do something," she whispered. "They'll freeze to death out there!"

He heard the *Englischer's* talking quietly by the front door. He poked his head around the edge of the door jamb, saw that Nate was helping Ripley with her coat. "Wait."

They looked down the hall at him.

"I don't think it's wise for you to go out there, especially in your wife's condition."

"Henry is right," Sadie stepped around him. "It's too cold out."

The *Englischers* exchanged a look. "But…"

"Why don't you spend the night here?" Sadie offered.

Henry looked at his wife and his heart nearly broke when she saw the brave smile she was wearing as she nodded at them. He knew how much personal cost that her words would come at, especially when Ripley's hands went to her distended belly.

He lent his voice to Sadie's. "Tomorrow, I'll take you in my buggy. We'll track down the phone, and then we'll see about helping with your car."

"We couldn't put you out," Ripley said, wide eyes going to Nate's.

"You're not," Sadie said. "It would take me a few minutes to make up the spare room. Please… I wouldn't sleep well knowing that we didn't do all we could to help you."

"That's a generous offer," Still, Nate hesitated. "If you're sure?"

"We are," Henry nodded. "In here, it's safe and warm."

"I can rustle up some food if you're hungry?" Sadie offered. "I have some potluck casserole that I can reheat."

Nate chuckled then. "Even before she was pregnant, Rip was always hungry. She's quite territorial over her food these days so you might regret the offer to cook for her."

His wife sent him a dark look, but Nate laughed and lay a hand around her shoulders, adding, "Said with the utmost love and respect, honey."

Ripley watched them both guardedly. "Are you sure we won't be putting you both out? I feel awful for having ruined your night already."

Henry's heart ached when Sadie walked up to the woman. Henry didn't know if she could withstand watching a pregnant Ripley around the house, but her Christian hospitality and upbringing pushed aside her misgivings.

He couldn't be prouder of her than right at this moment.

"How about a hot cocoa to warm you up?"

Ripley's dark eyes lit with pleasure. "Now you're talking my kind of language, Sadie."

They moved off down the hallway, the lamp light moving as they went.

Nate rubbed his hair. "Are you sure, man? This is… you don't even know us."

Henry unhooked his coat from where it hung on a peg by the door. "All strangers are friends we are yet to meet. Let me help fetch your bags from the car, then I propose we go and partake in cocoa. Sadie's hot chocolate is the best I've ever had."

RIPLEY

*S*adie's kitchen was warm and welcoming, with beautiful wooden cabinets and plain countertops polished to a shine. A sturdy table dominated the center of the room where the four of them sat. Ripley couldn't help but feel envy for the organization and simplicity of the room. Labeled jars lined the shelves. Pots of herbs filled the windowsill.

Sadie moved with practiced efficiency, her movements knowing and sure. Ripley couldn't help but wonder what it would be like to have grown up in a house like this.

Henry's claim that Sadie's hot chocolate was the best had been absolutely correct, and Sadie had indulged her with a second mug that Ripley gratefully wrapped her hands around.

The casserole had been delicious, and Sadie even added some freshly made bread in a basket alongside a colorful bowl of pickled vegetables.

"That was delicious," Ripley announced. "I didn't know how famished I was until I started eating." Ripley beamed from ear to ear at their hostess, who smiled shyly at her. "You're a wonderful cook. I've never been much of one, though I'd love to learn one day."

"Your *mamm* didn't teach you?"

Ripley was prepared for the familiar sting of embarrassment, though her rosy cheeks from the warmth of the stove meant that the feeling was inside only, not out for all the world to see.

Sadie must have sensed the hesitation because she quickly said, "I'm sorry, I didn't mean to pry."

Ripley felt compelled to explain. After all, this kind woman had opened up her home to her. "My childhood wasn't exactly what you'd call conventional. My mom had a lot of issues that impacted all of us kids. She did the best she could, but, well, there was an awful lot we had to figure out for ourselves," Ripley ran her hands across her stomach, reaffirming that long-ago promise that this child would never have to be the one to wrap their own Christmas gifts.

"That must have been difficult," Sadie's voice was filled with quiet compassion.

Ripley nodded. "We managed. Ferris, my older brother, stepped in when Mom was struggling. He owns his own business now cleaning pools. Gecko works in IT, Axel is training to be a nurse—much to the hilarity of his brothers—and Judd drives a truck. I always think it's a miracle that we all turned out the way we did."

"*Gott* is good," Henry murmured.

"Amen," Nate echoed.

Ripley wasn't sure it had anything to do with God. There were many times in her life when she felt her faith rocked, but she kept her comments to herself.

"Are you still in touch with your mother?" Henry asked her.

"Not much until recently," Ripley said. "We've had a strange relationship over the years. It was one of the reasons I wasn't bothered about going home for the holidays, but, you see, my mom is pretty sick at the moment and Nate was the one to point out to me that Mom wouldn't always be around."

Ripley, all too aware that her rambling had revealed far too much of herself, flicked her eyes to Nate and he gave her an amused shake of his head.

"Your mother is poorly?" Henry asked her.

"Yes. She has cancer."

Sadie made a sound of regret. "I'm sorry. I shall pray for her tonight."

Ripley smiled. She hadn't prayed in too long, and certainly not for helping the woman whose chaos had impacted her life so much. Still, Sadie didn't know this. "Thank you. How about you? Are your family close by?"

They each nodded. "Henry's family is large. Eleven of them," Sadie smiled.

Ripley's eyes bugged out. "Eleven? Goodness!"

"Yes," Henry grinned. "Plus, they all have many kinner—that is, children. Poor Sadie here is overwhelmed by it all."

"There's only my *schwester* and me, you see."

"*Schwester*?"

"Sorry, it means 'sister'," Sadie amended. "My dad passed when I was young. We grew up around here. I've known Henry all my life."

"And now you're married," Ripley smiled. "How wonderful."

"Yes," Sadie replied. "We've been married just over a year now."

"Four years for us," Nate said. "And now a baby to make it complete."

Ripley sensed rather than saw the reaction Nate's words caused. Sadie stood abruptly, her back to the room as she walked to the sink. Ripley tried not to look at her too closely. *Was she crying?*

Henry stood up. "Why don't I show you both to your room?"

"We should help you clear away all these plates," Nate said.

"Nonsense," Henry said. "Guests don't clear away."

"Okay, then. Thank you," Nate must have sensed the sudden tension in the room because concern creased his face. "Thank you for the delicious food, Sadie."

"That's okay," the woman said over her shoulder, sparing him a glance though not looking at them.

Henry chatted amicably as he led them through the house and up the stairs. There were no adornments. No photos or pictures on the walls. Just simple, rustic touches – framed embroidered bible sayings and beautiful hand-made quilts.

"Here you go," Henry opened the door and stepped back to allow them in. He'd placed their bags at the foot of the plain wooden bed that took up most of the space within the simple room. A stunning blue and green quilt covered the bed. Just like the rest of the house, there were no other adornments in the room other than what would be practical for them to use. A dresser and a wardrobe, a plain wooden chair.

Henry set the lamp on the bedside table. "You turn this dial to extinguish the light. There is no bathroom up here so be careful on the stairs if you have to use it in the night."

"Thank you for all your help," Ripley said.

"We're glad we could be of help," Henry replied with a smile. He paused in the doorway. "Don't rush up in the morning. Your car is far enough off the road not to cause an obstruction."

"Goodnight," Nate said.

"*Gut* night. Sleep well."

Neither of them moved as Henry's footsteps faded. Ripley was the first to move. She gingerly sat on the edge of the bed, surprised by how comfortable it felt.

"Are you feeling okay?"

She gave him a tired smile. "I'm a bit achy."

"Where?"

"Just my back, honey," she said, letting out a low moan of relief when Nate sat next to her on the bed and began to rub her lower back. "That feels good," she breathed.

"Was it me, or was something wrong with Sadie?"

Ripley lay her head on her shoulder, eyes drifting closed as she concentrated on the relief his hand was bringing about. "No, it wasn't you.

"I can only hope I didn't offend her."

Worry nibbled at her. She felt just as terrible as Nate that they might have upset their host. "She's shy but there's something else there. I don't think she was offended but..." She shrugged. "Maybe it's just my suspicious nature," she added.

Nate dropped a kiss on her crown. "They're nice, though, aren't they?"

She nodded. "Very. I'm ashamed to admit I didn't know much about the Amish. I put my foot in it earlier when I asked if they'd had a power cut."

Nate sniggered. "Rip, you didn't, did you?"

"Mm-hmm, I did. Plus, she's never seen a movie. She said she'd seen an episode of Friends one time in a hotel she was in."

"They're Amish. No modern conveniences," Nate said. "No cars. They use horses and buggies to get about, although will travel on buses and trains. They live simply, using and making as much as they can off the land. They use generators if they need power. Some communities are stricter about modernization than others."

She craned her neck to look at him. "How is it that you know so much about them?"

He chuckled. "I don't know a lot about them, honey. I just happen to know a little about how they live from reading and stuff. You ought to watch something other than *Grey's Anatomy*."

She thumped his leg half-heartedly. Nate kissed her cheek. "Come on, you must be exhausted."

She was shivering by the time she put on her pajamas and climbed into the bed. Nate let her get herself settled next to him, her head on his shoulder. His hand went to her stomach.

"You wake me if you need to use the toilet," he whispered, the house around them silent. Not tomb-like. Just comfortable. "I don't need you taking a sleepy tumble."

Ripley nodded, though she had no intention of waking him. He was just as exhausted as she, having worked extra in the run up to their break. Plus, he'd driven them.

Ripley shifted uncomfortably on the bed. The casserole was delicious but was now causing hellfire in her belly.

"Are you alright?"

"Yeah, just a little heartburn."

"That's what you get for having two cups of cocoa," he reminded her.

She poked him in the side. "One for me, one for the baby."

"I'm going to buy you a mug with that on," he murmured.

"You only have to put up with it for another few weeks."

His free hand went to her belly again. "I can't wait."

"The Weavers are like a Godsend. I thought we would spend the night in the car. How wonderful it is that they allowed strangers so different from them to stay overnight."

"Yeah. I can't tell you how grateful I am that you have a roof over your head, warm food in your belly and for our baby, too, and a nice warm bed."

She laughed softly. "You think we'll be able to sort the car? It's Christmas Eve tomorrow."

"Hmm?" Nate was already starting to drift.

Ripley smiled in the darkness. He'd always been able to drop off on command, something that she envied him. Moments later, she felt his body relax and his breathing evened out.

She closed her eyes, trying the breathing technique that she'd learned in the baby classes. The ache in her back was still there.

She figured it was probably from sitting in the car for quite a while from New York.

Nothing to worry about.

With that thought, she closed her eyes.

SADIE

"*A*men," Sadie said as Henry rounded off their night prayers. She combed her blonde hair before she climbed into bed beside her husband.

"You're quiet, my love," Henry asked after she made herself comfortable in bed.

Sadie turned her head on the pillow, looking at her husband. For a moment, she didn't trust her voice. Her throat ached from holding back the well of emotion that longed to burst free.

Henry's sigh was soft and full of sadness. "I wasn't sure about offering them shelter for the night, but it didn't seem right to send them on their way. If I'd known it was going to upset you this much, I wouldn't have made the offer in the first place."

Sadie reached for her husband's hand and said quickly, "No, no. You did absolutely the right thing. I meant what I said when I wouldn't have slept knowing that they were outside sitting in the car. Her pregnant no less," her voice cracked, and she pressed her trembling lips together.

Henry moved across the bed, the covers rustling as he carefully drew her into his arms.

"Come now," he told her gently. "The time will be right for us eventually."

Sadie wanted to believe his words, but she was unable to stop the words that left her mouth. "When? *When* will it be our time, Henry?"

Henry's arms tightened around her. "It's not our way to question *Gott's* plan. We must give thanks for whatever situation we find ourselves in. Tonight, we were meant to offer sustenance and shelter to two people in need. We don't know why they knocked on our door out of everyone's here."

"Because we were the only ones with lights on," Sadie suggested with a watery relief.

Henry clicked his tongue. "There's my girl,

always able to find something to laugh about." He released a heavy sigh. "I'm sure they knew how upset you were when they were going upstairs."

Regret and shame pinched her. "I couldn't help it," she whispered harshly. "We were also meant to become a family by now but, alas, it wasn't meant to be. Maybe it won't ever be for us."

She felt Henry still and he propped himself up on one elbow, gazing down into her watery eyes. "Why are you saying this?"

"It's true, Henry." Tears spilled from the sides of her eyes, trickling down her temples and into her hair. "Not only did we lose our *boppli,* but I also haven't been able to conceive again ever since. What if *Gott* is punishing me for something that I've done?"

Henry gasped as if he'd never seen her before. This only made Sadie feel more awkward. Perhaps he now realized what a mistake he had made in marrying her in the first place.

For as long as she could remember, Henry had been in her life. The Weavers were a large and boisterous family so everyone in their community knew them. She'd always known that he was the one she wanted to marry, even when other girls had flirted with him at Sunday Singing. The day he had asked her to marry him had been the most joyous of her life, until the day she was able to call him her husband. After then, it had been the day she'd found out their union had been blessed with a child.

"What possible sin could you have committed that would take away the life of an innocent baby?" His hand curved around her cheek, his thumb grazing the skin in a gentle caress. "My love, please don't feel this way."

"I'm a failure," Sadie blurted out. "A failure as a wife and as a mother."

Sighing, he gathered her into his arms and waited while the sobs wracked her body. "You could never fail me, Sadie Weaver. You are the light of my life and I have never been prouder of you than tonight when you opened our home to Ripley and Nate, even knowing that having a pregnant woman under your roof would make you feel deeply uncomfortable. You have a big heart, and you are kind and genuine. And I love you no matter whether we are blessed with a child or not. I will love you until my very last breath," he brushed strands of hair from her face. "Please have faith. Trust in Him that He has a plan for us. Don't blame yourself when you did nothing wrong."

She was envious, she thought.

She was not meant to covet what others had. Perhaps that was her sin. Or maybe it was because she had wallowed in her happiness. Perhaps that was why their attempts for another baby hadn't been successful. She turned her face away from his earnest gaze.

"Sadie, I mean it," Henry urged her.

Sadie sniffed and moved away from him to gaze up with wet eyes. "I can't help it. I tried to be strong and hopeful for both of us, but when I see pregnant women and children playing about, I get so sad because I can't give you a child of your own. I see you with your nieces and nephews, with the other children when we go to sermons on a Sunday. I know how much you love children."

"But I love you more," Henry told her fiercely.

"You deserve a child of your own," she cried. "I want so much to be able to do that for you."

Henry studied her for a moment. His quiet contemplation of her made her feel self-conscious. "No, don't look away," he pulled her chin back. "This is what you've been wrestling with all these past months?"

Sadie could only nod, evading his probing look.

"You never said a word to me."

"What good would it have done? It was your loss, too. I saw how much it hurt you."

"You must never feel that you have to hide anything from me. Didn't we make this promise to each other a year ago?" He brushed a gentle kiss to her mouth. "Your burden is my burden, Sadie. I feel wretched that you've carried this all alone, but you did nothing wrong to cause the loss of our child."

Sadie's swallow was audible in the silence of the room. She so desperately wanted to believe him. He wiped away her tears, his thumbs coarse against her soft cheek. "*Liebchen*, I need you to understand that this was not your fault. It just wasn't meant to be. Mrs. Kaufman explained all of this to you on that terrible night. Did she not tell us about the many women in the community who have been in this situation and went on to have healthy children?"

Reluctantly, Sadie nodded. "She did, yes."

"Do you love me?"

"Oh Henry, yes. More with each passing day."

"And I feel the same. All that matters is that we are together. You make me so happy. We will have a wonderful Christmas, surrounded by *familye*."

Sadie knew then that she was very blessed already in her husband. His faith – in Gott, in her, in their marriage – buoyed hers.

"Now sleep," he stroked her cheek and kissed her on the mouth once more. "And we shall see what tomorrow brings us."

RIPLEY

*W*ith a small groan, Ripley stirred awake.

She tried to change her position on the bed, but she felt so heavy, she could hardly move a muscle. The room was cold.

Had the furnace gone out?

Had her mom not paid the bill again?

She opened her eyes, blinking into the blackness. For a moment, she became disconcerted by her strange surroundings. Where were the streetlights? She reached for the bedside lamp and felt nothing.

Alarm rose inside, then she remembered the strange house and the kind couple who'd taken them in. The dull ache in her back forced her to try and move. The lance of pain through her middle forced a gasp from her.

Again, she tried moving but felt as if she'd swallowed a whale.

Her hand struck out, and reassurance flooded her when she felt the warm form of Nate. She tried rolling to assuage the ache, and the pain shot through her again. This time, it was strong enough to steal her breath, bringing tears to her eyes.

Fear – white-hot and real – filled her.

Not again.

"Nate," she whispered.

Her husband didn't move. A vice tightened around her stomach, and she had to hold her breath through it.

"Nate," she gasped, when her stomach was no longer rock hard. She reached out to shake him. *"Nathan!"*

"Hmm?"

"Wake up!"

"What is it, honey? Do you need help to go to the bathroom?"

Trying to hold back the rising panic inside her, she whispered, "Something's wrong."

The bed rocked as he moved. "What do you mean?"

"I don't know," she whimpered. "Something… it hurts."

His hand reached for her, and she gripped his hand tightly. "Turn on the light."

She listened as he fumbled for the lamp. It dinged and clattered but to no avail. "There's no… Hold on a sec."

She heard the sound of his belt hit the wooden floor as he grabbed his jeans. Moments later, his phone screen illuminated the room. She squinted as he aimed it at her.

"You're all sweaty, Rip."

She held a hand to shield her eyes from the brightness. "My stomach keeps tightening. And my back, the ache hasn't gone away all night."

Nate tutted at her. "Why didn't you wake me sooner?" He fiddled with the lamp and the soft light glowed gently around the room.

"Because an aching back is normal when you're carrying another human," she snapped at him. "I don't wake you at every niggle. Growing a human is a natural thing to do."

"All right," he scooted off the edge of the bed and stepped into his pants, fastening the buttons as he padded around the foot of it. "Try sitting up. It might be that you're not used to this mattress."

Ripley wanted to snap again at him and tell him it was a ridiculous notion when the bed was perfectly comfortable, but her belly tightened again. She moaned and groaned.

"Are you in labor?"

"I don't know," she wailed as he helped her into a sitting position. "I've never been in labor before."

Nate squatted in front of her, resting his hands on her thighs as she panted from the exertion of sitting up. "Should I call an ambulance?"

Ripley waited for the wave of pain to subside enough to be able to speak. "How? We're here because we have no cell reception."

"A doctor then," Nate suggested, unfazed by her waspish tone. "They must have a local one."

"I can't be in labor. I'm not due for another month."

"It's just under three weeks, honey," Nate said. "It's fine. Just try to stay calm."

She knew he was trying to help but the tears came anyway. "I'm scared, Nate."

At her words, Nate stirred into action. He cupped her face and kissed her moist forehead. "Nothing will happen to our baby. Maybe it's just a false alarm. Remember the nurses in the birth classes told us about false labor?" He waited for her nod. "It's probably just that. Your body getting ready for delivering. Everything will be fine."

Ripley leaned into his touch. She didn't want to have her baby here in the middle of nowhere. She wanted a clean hospital, surrounded by experienced staff and the calming voice of her very capable OBGYN.

She hadn't even wanted to go to Cleveland in the first place.

If he'd have done as she'd asked, they'd be at home.

She'd have the phone on the nightstand.

There'd be an ambulance on the way.

She could have her doctor on the phone with her, coaching her through this terror. Instead, she was sat in a strange house with no contact to the outside world and their only mode of transport was abandoned somewhere outside.

She was only here because Nate had guilted her into thinking about her mom not being here next year.

"What?" He asked.

She stared at him. It wasn't his fault that he

was the eternal optimist. She'd known that when she married him. "Nothing."

His sigh told her exactly what he thought of her rehearsed answer. "This isn't a sign that you weren't meant to go and see your mom, Rip."

Her lips twitched in response to him knowing exactly her train of thought. "Don't do that. You know how much I hate it when you do that."

He sat on the edge of the bed. "Your mom has been trying to make amends with you, to right all the wrongs she did. Gecko and Judd have a good relationship with her. Even Axel has forgiven her. They all say how much she is trying to stay clean and sober."

"They were too young to see much of it. Ferris and I did our best to shield them all."

He laid an arm over her shoulders and kissed her temple. "I know you did. The same as I also know that deep down you want to be able to forgive her. Everyone deserves a second chance."

Ripley wanted to remind him that her mom had used up multiple chances over the years, but it was true that she'd been clean and sober.

And that took courage. Axel had been the one to come to his siblings to plead their mother's case. Gecko and Judd had been quick to capitulate. Only Ferris and Ripley remained obstinately steadfast in their reluctance to let their mom back in their lives.

Because she'd let them down so often in the past.

She flapped a hand as the tightening started again. "I'm not talking about my mom right now," she said crossly. "There are much more important things going on."

"Is it happening again?"

Pained, Ripley could only nod.

"They're fairly regular, huh?"

She nodded, again.

"I want to get you checked out." He turned for the neat pile of clothes she'd folded on the chair in the corner.

"Where? You said the Amish don't have hospitals."

He closed his eyes for a moment to think. They popped back open. "That's true, but they have midwives and... and... we'll get you there."

"How?" Ripley asked again, trying not to be pessimistic, but her trepidation was rising at the seeming hopelessness of their situation. "Listen to that wind. I bet it's still snowing out, too."

Nate handed her a t-shirt to put on. "If I have to walk miles in the snow to get a doctor or midwife from anywhere, I will."

She threaded her arms through the armholes and smiled up at him. "My hero."

He quickly performed a Superman-style pose. "Not all heroes wear capes."

Ripley couldn't help chuckling at his words. She knew Nate would move mountains just to make her happy. "Are you going to put your shorts on the outside of your pants next?"

Nate chuckled and dropped a quick kiss on her head. "In pain and still making terrible jokes, I see. Lift your foot." He quickly put on her socks for her. "Surely, over the years, some women must have gone into labor in such weather. I'm sure that the people around here have made available solutions for such a situation."

Her bottom lip wobbled as her racing thoughts lurched ahead. Ripley fought to look on the bright side, but she still couldn't. She was afraid there might be no happy ending for them. After all, happiness had been in short supply in her world all along. The nagging feeling that all wasn't well with her baby for wanting to come early wouldn't go away.

"Nate," she reached for his hand. "What if…"

Nate, sensing her distress, took her hand and kissed it. "Don't worry, honey. By the time our baby is ready to come, you'll have all the help you need."

Tears rolled down her face. "I'll never forgive myself if something bad happens to our baby."

"Don't think like that, honey." He smiled, even though it looked strained. "Think of how extra special our Christmas celebrations will be when we celebrate our baby's birthday every year."

Ripley tried to look optimistic, but she couldn't. She kept on imagining the worst. When she winced from the pain shooting up her back, Nate's hold tightened on her hand.

"I'll go wake Henry. He'll know how to reach the midwife. Perhaps he will use his buggy to go and get her. Yes… I'm sure he'll do that."

She shook her head. "Please don't leave me. I don't want to be on my own."

He kissed her hand. "You won't be alone. Sadie will be with you."

"But I don't know her. I want *you* with me."

He cupped her chin. "Ripley, I can't allow Henry to go out there alone. He might come back if the midwife can't come with him, but I'll won't stop until I find someone to come back here and help you."

She nodded at his logical explanation, even though she couldn't bear the thought of him out there in the snow and cold.

"Please be strong for me and our baby. Everything will be fine, I promise." His hand tightened on hers for a second before he kissed her and scrambled off the bed.

Her strangled gasp stopped him in his tracks. He turned back. "Rip?"

There was an unexpected sensation below, a gushing that she couldn't control. Suddenly, the throbbing pain increased. She raised wide eyes to his.

Something was wrong.

"I think my water just broke."

They stared at each other for a moment, Nate's eyes popping open as her words had the desired effect. He wrenched open the bedroom and bellowed, "*Help!* Henry! Sadie! Please, we need some help!"

Watching him leave the room was one of the hardest things Ripley had ever done. She knew that she could rely on him. He wouldn't stop until he had found someone who could help them, even to the detriment of his health.

She listened to the voices carry through the silent house, the strange accent of their hosts as they answered Nate's desperate pleas.

She placed her hands against her stomach and took a deep breath. "Please stay in there a while longer, little one," she whispered. "I want to meet you too, so much, but it's too soon yet. I couldn't bear to lose you, not now." Ripley closed her eyes as tears spilled from the edges down her face. She couldn't remember the last time she prayed, but right now, it was the only thing she could think to do.

"Lord, I'm so sorry I've not spoken to you in a long while. I know that I haven't been the best person I could be. I've tried to live a kind life. I've tried to do my best… do unto others as I wish done to me. I know that I've doubted. Doubted in You.

"Please don't hold that against me as I come to you now for help." She sniffed heavily.

"Please help me. Please don't allow anything to happen to my baby. *Please.*"

Sobs wracked her body because she knew she didn't deserve an answer from God, having lost her way all these years.

She could only hope He would forgive her and have mercy on her and her baby.

NATE

*T*he winds kicked up the snow across the frozen landscape, blurring the world around them. Snow whipped against Nate's face, stinging his skin despite the scarf that Henry had loaned him. It was hardly surprising that there wasn't a soul about. The late hour and the inclement weather had everyone battening down the hatches to wait out the storm.

The beams of the small battery-operated torches did very little against the swirling storm that howled around them like a living thing. Nate huddled deeper into his coat, trying to make out the rutted tracks of the road amongst the whirling drifts.

Henry was bundled up in a heavy coat, with

a black felt hat pulled down low. The brim kept the snow out of his eyes as it slapped at them both.

Harnessing the horse had been quicker than he thought it would take, though still not as fast as simply jumping in the car and starting the engine. However, now they were moving faster than Nate would have dared in a car under these conditions, the horse's surefooted-ness cutting through drifts that would have surely stranded a vehicle.

Perhaps there was more to be said for this mode of transport after all.

Nate gripped the bench he sat on as they passed his marooned vehicle, a forlorn lump of useless metal now buried under a thick blanket of snow.

The horse moved forward with practiced ease; its breath visible in puffs of steam. Henry handled the buggy with steady hands, his posture calm and assured as though they were not battling the elements of a ferocious storm. His gloved hands flicked lightly, guiding the horse along the invisible ribbon of road. Nate couldn't be sure where the edge of the road was and was thankful for Henry's capability.

"Is it far?" Nate had to shout to be heard over the roar of the wind.

"Not too far!" Henry shouted back. "Just on the other side of town. It will take around twenty minutes at this pace."

Nate had to tamp down on the rising panic in his chest. "Do you think Mrs. Kauffman will come? We're not Amish... What if she isn't there?"

Henry offered him a reassuring grin, turning slightly to meet his eyes. "Do not worry. Mrs. Kauffman has delivered many babies in this area, including *Englischer* babies. She is a kind soul and sees all as *Gott's* children."

"And if she's not there?" Nate pressed. The image of Ripley's silent plea in her wide, fear-filled eyes as he'd left clutched at his heart. She'd been trying her best to hold it together, self-conscious in front of Sadie because of the mess she'd made on the other woman's pristine bedlinen.

"Mrs. Kauffman has two daughters who are also trained to help mothers bring their children into the world. We will not leave there without help. Trust in *Gott*, Nate."

The quiet confidence in the man's words

steadied Nate a little, and he tried to hold onto that feeling. The thought of his wife, alone and scared, didn't help. He had hated leaving her, but he'd had no choice. The buggy jolted when it bounced over a hidden obstacle in the road, and Nate had to brace himself. Henry didn't slow down, calm and confident as always, his actions precise and sure.

"I really appreciate all you're doing," Nate called out. "I'm sorry if we've interrupted any plans you had."

"We are happy to help you both," Henry replied, steering around a second abandoned vehicle. "Mrs. Kauffman is very good. You'll see."

"You know her well then?"

Henry hesitated, though it was not to concentrate on what he was doing. "Sadie and I..."

Nate turned to him when he trailed off and he saw a flash of deep sadness pass over the other man's face. The storm momentarily forgotten; Nate shook his head with under-standing. "Sorry, man, you don't have to explain."

"It's fine," Henry said. "We lost our first child

last summer. Sadie miscarried when she was four months along."

Nate could only stare. The sadness from earlier, Sadie's reaction in the kitchen—he reached under his glasses to rub his eyes, biting back the groan. No wonder Sadie had reacted the way she did to his comment. "Henry, that's terrible. I'm so sorry."

Henry flicked a look at him. "We were ecstatic at the good news, of course. To be blessed so soon after we'd married. She started bleeding one day. No cause. No falls or anything like that. We tried everything we could, but we lost our *boppli*."

"It doesn't help you much, I know, But I do understand what you've been through," Nate offered. "Rip and I... We've had our own issues. It's taken four years to get to this point. She's been pregnant before, and we've lost every baby. We could only afford one round of IVF. It failed. She was beside herself. We... we almost split up," Nate moved his mouth, his throat tightening over the words he so rarely admitted even to himself. "She was angry and a little self-destructive. We gave up trying, if only while we repaired our marriage. The next thing you know, she was pregnant naturally. It was like the IVF had reminded her body what it was supposed to be doing.

"At first, we didn't dare hope. We made it past the first trimester but didn't tell a soul. We'd made that mistake in the past, you see. Then once we had the growth scan, we started to plan." His voice cracked, and he dug his thumbs into his eye sockets again, this time to stave off the tears. Thinking of Ripley clutching her belly and battling pain brought another wave of panic through him. "And now this."

"You're doing everything you can for Ripley and your baby. They'll be fine."

"I hope so, Henry," Nate pushed his glasses up his nose. "If something happens to either of them, I'm not sure I'll survive. I really wish I had your faith."

"Your story fills me with hope, my friend," Henry leaned down. "Thank you for sharing it. Sadie took the loss much harder than I thought. Having you here tonight has pushed us to face it. *Gott* has been our strength but having you here has been a blessing for us."

Gratitude filled Nate and he smiled at the other man, a feeling of affinity passing between them both. "Sometimes, it's hard being the man. We don't go through the physical loss, of course, but it's a loss nonetheless."

Henry met his eyes briefly. He nodded. "Our women are strong, Nate. We are blessed."

"Yes, we are."

"Ripley and your baby are in His hands. It will be fine, for sure and certain."

They passed through the sleepy town that was eerily quiet, the buildings cloaked in dustings of snow, glittering under the hazy glow of the streetlights. The road stretched ahead, blanketed in pristine white. They moved past the town proper and rounded a bend, with a further scattering of houses visible through the storm. Like Henry and Sadie's house, a few other windows held the soft glow of candlelight.

The Kauffman house was a large, sturdy structure surrounded by several outbuildings and a stable. Dogs barked to announce their arrival, so that by the time Henry had come to a stop in the fenced yard, and stamped up the steps onto the sheltered porch, lamplight glowed in the downstairs.

The front door was opened, revealing a young blonde woman, wrapped in a shawl. Her face was illuminated by the lamp she held aloft.

She was much younger than Nate had expected, though her expression was calm and curious. Her gaze swept over the bedraggled men, as if having people arrive at her door in the middle of the night was a regular occurrence.

"Henry Weaver? Is that you?"

Henry hailed her. "Is your *mamm* home, Rebecca? We have a house guest in urgent need of her services."

The interested gaze settled on Nate. "My wife," he explained quickly. "Her waters have broken, but her due date is still three weeks away."

"*Ach*, a *boppli* will come when it is ready, not a moment sooner," Rebecca rolled her eyes. "Wait in here. I shall go and wake up *Mamm*."

Nate copied Henry and tapped off the snow from his boots before he stepped inside. The interior of the farmhouse was cozy simplicity. Rebecca had disappeared, her moccasin slippers slapping softly against the gleaming wooden floors. A fire glowed pleasantly in the wide hearth, and a half-finished embroidery project sat on the plump sofa. Just like the Weaver's house, the furniture was sturdy and well-made, yet practical. The room smelled of lavender and woodsmoke.

Nate wanted to pace. The ball of energy nipping at his heels.

Ripley.

All alone.

His baby.

"What's taking them so long?"

Henry, composed and unflustered, laid a hand on his shoulder. "She'll come. Sadie is with Ripley. Mrs. Kauffman is the best in the area."

Nate sighed heavily, his gaze flicking around the room.

"Are you a man who prays?"

Nate looked at Henry. "Yes, sir, I am."

"Then let's pray together," Henry offered.

Nate could only nod. They bowed their heads, standing side by side, as Henry's calm voice carried softly between them, making a gentle, heartfelt plea for strength and guidance.

Nate added a silent plea of his own.

Please, Lord, let us be in time.

SADIE

SEVEN MONTHS EARLIER

MORE THAN A THIRD of pregnancies end in miscarriage.

MRS. KAUFFMAN'S words were meant to comfort her. To explain that what had happened to her the day before wasn't her fault.

At first, it had only been a twinge. Her body had been changing shape. By the time the midwife had arrived, Sadie had only had to look at her face to know that her worst fears had been realized.

Henry had been at the workshop. The memory of his grief-stricken face would forever be etched into her mind. He'd rushed into the house and had scooped her up. He'd wept with her, cradling her as if she was spun glass.

The house felt empty, the loss all that much greater because their hopes and dreams had evaporated before their eyes.

She sat on the swing Henry had presented to her only the week before. A beautiful hand-made gift for her to sit out and watch the fireflies from their porch in the summer evenings. She didn't swing on it.

May had unfurled across the land. Her garden teemed with her efforts, flowers and vegetables exploding from the soil.

Tall spikes of lupines swayed in the light winds, their vibrant shades of pinks and purples standing above the elegant petals of the lavender and yellow irises. Peonies were beginning to bloom next to them. Marigolds popped out next to where the cabbages and lettuces were emerging through the dark soil in neat rows. Pansies, columbines, snapdragons... why had she bothered to plant any of them? None of it mattered now.

The sweet scent of blossoms scented the air that glided over her, stirring the strands of her blonde hair around her jawline. Crossly, she swiped at it.

She wanted to scream, to rave at the unfairness of it all.

But that was not their way, was it?

What she really wanted was undeniable proof that Mrs. Kauffman and Henry were right. That it wasn't her fault. Because, right now, it felt like she was being punished.

She'd been too happy. She'd been too ecstatic.

She'd had everything she'd ever wanted – a home, a husband, and a family.

It was wrong to gloat. Yet that was what she'd done.

And this was *Gott's* way of reminding her that she had to remain humble.

The screen door squealed. Henry paused in the doorway, tutting angrily as he frowned at the offending hinge. She heard him mutter something unintelligible, then he let the door go. It slapped back against the house noisily. He crossed to the railing that he'd added to the edge of the porch and rested his forearms on it.

He looked out across the garden. He rubbed his beard thoughtfully, then dragged his hands down his face. The sorrow that creased his face broke her heart.

When she stood up, he straightened and whirled, startled. He quickly schooled his face and offered her a gentle smile.

"I thought you'd gone for a lie down, *Liebchen*."

"I tried but I could not rest," she said as she crossed to where he stood. She rested her hip against the rail, looked out across the garden.

He felt it, too, she acknowledged. That, at least, brought her comfort to know that she was not alone. And as his wife, she needed to be strong for him. For them. She watched the bees flit from flower to flower. Birds swoop through the air, riding on the warm airflow.

Their way was not to dwell on hardships, but to trust in *Gott's* way. To find peace in His wisdom.

Henry turned to her then. Wordlessly, he drew her to his side. She tucked herself under his arm, resting her head against him.

The warm sun bathed her face. She tilted

her face up, welcomed in the light. And prayed for the strength to get through the next day.

"*Gott's* plan doesn't always make sense to us," Henry whispered. "but one day it will. I know it. And if not, we still have each other. We just have to be patient."

She nodded, not trusting herself to speak.

PRESENT DAY.

SADIE LEANED on against her kitchen counter.

The wind raged still. The snow flurries swirled against the window. The sky was beginning to lighten. Not much, but enough that she could make out the dark shapes of the outbuildings in the yard.

The memory of that summer's day faded as she blinked, trying to clear her thoughts. She didn't often allow herself to dwell on that awful day, nor the blur that had followed. For too long, Sadie had had to pretend that she was okay.

She'd picked up her needlework. She'd pushed the needle through the material to finish the green and blue quilt she'd started for their child. She'd carefully wrapped it and given it Anna-Mary Beiler instead.

She'd tended to her garden, coaxing the vegetables and herbs from the soil, then turned them into delicious meals that had nourished their bodies.

She'd attended the Sunday services. She'd sung their songs. She'd gone through the motions, just like she was fine.

Because that was what was expected of her.

She didn't think about that day at all. She kept it locked carefully away. But the past hour had forced it back into her consciousness.

From Nate hammering on their door, with panic threaded through his voice. She understood that fear all too well. Henry had remained unruffled. He'd dressed quickly, reassuring the panicking *Englischer* that a buggy was the best way to get around in the snow.

Then they'd hurried outside, bundled up against the storm, leaving her alone with Ripley.

A very pregnant Ripley.

A very scared, pregnant woman who right now needed her help.

Sadie turned from the window. She

finished adding what was needed for the tea and carried it on a tray through her house and up the stairs.

Ripley was stood, her hands on the window ledge, leaning. "Where are they? Shouldn't they be back by now?" She asked without preamble.

"They shouldn't be too much longer," Sadie said as she set the tray down. "I made you some ginger tea. It will help with the nausea."

Ripley waited a moment longer before she straightened up. She pressed a hand to her back and waddled back over. Damp tendrils of her hair was stuck to her temples. "Thank you. And I'm sorry again about the bedding. I will replace them."

She had helped Ripley change her clothing and then quickly stripped and re-made the soiled bed. Having something practical to do had taken her mind off things. But now she must sit and wait and keep a close eye on her house guest. Sadie indicated that Ripley was to sit down on the bed. "They'll wash perfectly fine. You should save your money."

Ripley sat down heavily with a groan and accepted the cup. "Thank you. Mm, that smells delicious. Did your mom show you how to make this, too?"

"No," Sadie smirked. "That one is shop bought."

Ripley eyed her, amusement gleaming in them. "I thought the Amish made everything they ate."

"Who told you that?"

"Nate. He Googled it. On the internet," Ripley supplied helpfully.

"Oh. Well, we buy some things, especially if they're out of season, or it's easier," Sadie held a plate aloft. "These I made though. Ginger cookies. My *grossmammi's* recipe."

"*Grossmammi?*"

"Grandmother, on my father's side," Sadie sat on the chair in the corner.

"I never knew my grandparents. My dad took off when we were little. Left my mom to raise us alone," Ripley sipped at the cup. "Actually, she's probably wondering where we are."

"Henry will go find the community phone today," Sadie said. "You can call her then."

"Henry is a good man," Ripley said. "Nothing seems to bother him."

Sadie smiled fondly. "He grew up in a large family. They are a boisterous bunch. But *jah*, he's a very good man."

Ripley sucked in a sharp breath. "Another one," she said.

Sadie took the cup and then helped Ripley up, remembering what she'd said about how moving around helped with the pain.

"I bet you regret opening your front door last night, huh?" Ripley said, her breath huffing out on a dry laugh. "Especially considering how messed up your night has been."

Sadie turned with Ripley, walked back across the floor. "I have a feeling that you were sent to us," she said, helping Ripley onto the bed when she reached for it. "How's that?"

"Yeah, good," Ripley pulled herself higher up the bed. She pressed her hands to her stomach, and Sadie could see that she was fighting against the waves of pain.

"Just take deep breaths. Everything will be fine," Sadie placed another pillow behind her head.

"Are you sure, Sadie? My baby is about to come three weeks early. That's not normal." Ripley gazed at her with frantic eyes.

Sadie bowed her head for a moment, trying to find the right words to comfort her.

Sadie lifted her head and gave her guest a warm smile. "Maybe the doctor got the date wrong. I heard the date given isn't always accurate. My younger sister came three weeks earlier than we expected. My *mamm* delivered her with no hitches."

"Is that true? Or are you doing the thing where you tell a lie to make someone feel better?"

Sadie's smile widened. "I'm Amish. We don't lie."

Ripley fell back against the pillows, her laughter weak and helpless. "I hope you're right, Sadie. I don't know what I'd do if I lost this baby. I can't go through the pain of losing a baby again."

Sadie frowned. "What do you mean?"

Ripley sighed and shifted with obvious discomfort on the bed. "This isn't my first pregnancy. I've had multiple miscarriages. I even tried IVF. We'd already given up on having children when I discovered I was pregnant again."

Sadie took her hand and gripped it. Her heart ached in a very real way. "*Ach*, Ripley."

Ripley blinked twice before understanding bloomed in her expression. "You, too, huh?"

Sadie forced a smile. "I bought the ginger

tea last summer, to help me with my morning sickness."

Ripley's soft gasp of dismay made her eyes sting with fresh tears.

Sadie needed to swallow several times until her throat was less tight. "It happened in May. One time was painful enough but over and over again? Ripley, I cannot imagine such a thing."

"I thought there was something wrong with me," Ripley said. "I took drugs when I was younger. Part of my rebellious streak. I thought that..."

"That maybe you were being punished," Sadie finished for her. Hearing those words was like watching herself in a mirror. She'd said the exact same thing.

Ripley shifted on the bed again. "Stupid, huh? But your mind plays funny tricks on you when you're grieving."

Sadie sat back. "I'm sorry, Ripley."

"What are you apologizing for? It isn't your fault."

Sadie's eyes glistened with tears. "I was judgmental when I saw you were pregnant. I didn't understand why you would travel in your condition in this harsh weather. Why you would take such a risk." She lowered her wet eyes. "The thing is, I was jealous of you."

"Jealous?"

Sadie lifted her head and nodded, shame curling in her belly. "I've been trying to conceive since then without success. So, when I saw you earlier, my loss stared me hard in the face. I judged you unfairly and I'm sorry for it."

Ripley squeezed Sadie's hand. "Don't worry about it. I know the feeling very well. It's like being a failure at what others do successfully without batting an eyelid. I've judged every pregnant woman in the last five years, wondering why she got to be a mom and I didn't. I blamed God for the unfairness of it all. Then I fell pregnant, and I felt like I had to take it all back. Maybe it's the crazy pregnancy hormones or... oh, heck, I don't know. All I know is you don't need to say you're sorry to me, Sadie."

"Well, all right, then," Sadie nodded.

"Can I have some more of my tea?"

Sadie handed her the cup, picked up her own.

"Did you make this quilt?"

Sadie shook her head. "It was a wedding gift

from Sarah, one of Henry's sisters. I haven't made a quilt since… that is, I was making one."

"For your baby," Ripley reached for her hand. "I'm so sorry you lost your baby."

Sadie waited for the next bit.

Ripley simply smiled. "I won't tell you that it'll happen for you soon because I know that you won't believe me. And it might not happen for you at all. Telling you stuff I think you need to hear won't help."

And just like that, it felt as if a weight had been lifted off her chest.

Sadie could only nod. "Thank you for understanding."

Ripley shrugged and dipped for a drink of her tea.

Sadie could see the shimmer of tears brimming in her eyes.

Ripley cleared her throat. "Tell me about your wedding."

Sadie understood the need to have something else to focus on. "We were married in October after the harvest last year. We tend to get married later in the year, after the farming season so that our friends and *familye* are free to attend. It's a grand occasion," Sadie explained about the day, stopping only when

Ripley's contractions came. She told her about having the celery sticks in mason jars because of the importance in their culture.

In turn, Ripley told her about her unconventional wedding to Nate. Just a few friends and her brothers, exchanging their vows on the side of a half-frozen lake.

"I think I should have liked brothers," Sadie said. "Henry's family is large, and he had both *bruders* and sisters. There's just my sister and me."

Ripley shook her head. "No, growing up, all I wanted was a sister. My brothers were annoying as heck. They were messy and destructive. I remember one Christmas wishing that Santa would swap them for sisters," she smiled at the memory. "Of course, now, I wouldn't swap them for the world."

"They'll make good uncles," Sadie nodded.

Ripley's eyes watered again. "And that's why I'm so afraid. We've come so far. I don't want anything to happen to my baby."

Just like Ripley had done, Sadie didn't offer her any inane reassurances. When you'd been through what she had, they wouldn't mean a thing, not deep inside.

"You know earlier on," Ripley sniffed. "I was

thinking that Nate was wrong for pushing me to make this trip to see my mom. Like I told you over supper, my childhood wasn't great. It's been a long time coming to forgive my mom. But I think that I was meant to be here," Ripley rubbed the heel of her hand to her chest. "Do you ever get that feeling?"

A warmth bloomed in Sadie's chest, turning into a soft smile that slid across her face. "Indeed, I do. Which means that Henry was right. *Gott* works in mysterious ways. When the time is right, He will show us."

"Oh, no, no," Ripley shook her head playfully. "We never admit our husbands are right, Sadie. Even when they are, which is most of the time in Nate's case"

"We don't?"

Ripley waved her fingers between them. "You stick with me, my friend. I'll steer you right."

Sadie laughed, delighted in the new friendship that seemed to be growing between them. They had so much in common, even though their worlds were so far apart.

"Oh," Ripley grimaced and braced herself. "Here comes another one."

"It's okay, I've got you," Sadie knelt beside

her, holding Ripley's pained gaze as the pain rolled through her body. "You're not alone, Ripley. I'm right here with you."

Somewhere below them, they heard the front door open. They heard Nate bellowing her name. The thundering footsteps as he climbed the stairs two at a time. Seconds later, he burst into the door.

"Rip?"

"Nate!" Ripley sobbed, stretching her hands out to him. "Where have you been?"

Henry followed behind him, and bringing up the rear was the familiar face of Mrs. Kauffman.

"*Gott* be praised," Sadie whispered with pent-up relief.

RIPLEY

"**O**kay, Ripley," Rachel Kauffman said.

Despite having been woken up in the middle of the night and implored to leave her house in the icy weather to attend to someone outside her faith, the midwife was kindness itself. She was a calmly capable presence in the stuffy room, just what you needed on a night like this.

"I need one more big push and you'll be there."

Ripley wanted to give up.

She was exhausted and the pain was becoming too much. Lavender, geranium and arnica scented the air, herbs that Rachel had used to help with her laboring. After the midwife arrived and reassured Ripley that her labor was progressing smoothly, Ripley felt a wave of relief. However, she grew concerned when Sadie unexpectedly offered to assist the midwife. Nate and Henry had returned later than expected, as they had to take Rebecca, the midwife's daughter, back home due to another urgent call from a pregnant woman in the community. Sadie's willingness to step in and help took both Ripley and the midwife, Rachel, by surprise. She needn't have worried. Sadie had stayed right be her side the whole time, a source of support throughout.

Sadie nodded at her now, silently supporting her.

Rachel patted her knees, drawing her attention back to the matter at hand. "You're doing fantastic, *Liebchen*. You're nearly there, okay?"

Nate took the cloth that Sadie offered him and lay it against her damp forehead. It was instantly cooling, and she looked up gratefully. "That feels nice."

Nate knelt on the floor next to the bed, took her hand. His green gaze fixed on her face. "I'm right here with you. You *can* do this."

As always, he'd read her mind. If nothing else went well in her life, she knew that she'd won the husband awards the day she'd married him.

She gripped his hand as another contraction surged through her. The world around her narrowed until she saw only Nate, heard only the sounds of her ragged breathing. Pain rocked her. Her eyes snapped shut. In the storm that ravaged her body, she gripped on tightly to his hand. An anchor to her as she pushed with everything she had left. Her voice ripped into a raw cry as that one final push brought about a new sound in the room: the sharp indignant wail of a newborn.

Ripley's eyes flew open, as Rachel's hands moved swiftly. Sadie worked alongside her, following her directions without question as the midwife swaddled the wriggling bundle. The protesting wails increased, and a smiling Rachel looked over at them.

"Well, there's no doubt that she's here!"

"She?" Ripley asked, eyes shining as her heart bumped.

"*Jah*, you have a *dochder*," Rachel said. "You didn't know what you were having?"

"We opted out of finding out," Nate said, his eyes shining.

"There aren't many true surprises left in

this world," Ripley explained, her head collapsed back against the pillow.

"That's true enough," Rachel agreed.

Nate's laughter was thick with emotion. He kissed her forehead several times. "You hear that, Rip? A girl. You did it, honey."

Tears streamed down her face as a heady blend of joy and relief flooded through her. "I did, didn't I?"

"Mm-hmm," he grinned.

Ripley craned her neck to get a better look at her baby girl.

Rachel carefully stood and then placed the baby in her outstretched arms. "Your daughter, Mrs. Weaver. A strong and healthy – if a little small – baby girl."

Ripley stared down into the pink, scrunched up face. Her daughter frowned up at her as if she, too, couldn't quite work out how she was here so soon. She had a tiny button nose and a dusting of dark hair. "She's perfect," Ripley whispered thickly.

Nate kissed his wife. "You're perfect."

"We'll give you a few minutes alone," Rachel said.

Just before the door closed, Ripley caught Sadie's eye. The other woman was wreathed in smiles, a happy light shining in her eyes. Ripley mouthed her thanks and then the door closed.

"I can't believe she's here," Ripley stroked the rose-bud cheeks with the edge of her forefinger.

"How do you feel?"

"Tired," she admitted. "But also, so very happy."

"Me, too. I wasn't sure we'd make it back in time. You're right. We should have put off visiting your mom until the new year. It was stupid of me to fetch you out."

Ripley shook her head. "No, it was right that I was here tonight."

Nate gestured at the curtains. Bright morning light edged them. "Last night now."

Ripley gave a tired laugh. "Last night, then. I just know that we were meant to be stop here, with these people."

Nate pulled back, his brow lifting as he regarded her. "Divine intervention, Rip?"

She clicked her tongue and swatted his shoulder. "You can scoff all you like, Nate."

"It's not scoffing. I feel it, too."

Ripley turned her attention back to the tiny bundle in her arms. She wasn't ready to admit out loud to her husband that she'd sought help from God last night.

"We need a name for her," Ripley said.

"I thought you'd already picked Isabella?"

Ripley shook her head. "I changed my mind." The door handle rattled before it opened.

Rachel's head appeared around the edge. "How are you doing?"

"Good, though she's scowling at me," Ripley said with a laugh.

"*Ach*, that's normal," Rachel smiled.

Sadie followed the midwife in. "I'm just fetching some tea and food for you, then I'm going," she said hurriedly.

"Actually, I'm glad you're here," Ripley said. She glanced at Nate, then looked back at Sadie. She beckoned her closer. "I want you to meet Sadie Kimberly Campbell."

Sadie went still as she stared at them both.

Ripley gazed down into her daughter's face. "I want her to have a name that means something to me."

Her wide eyes filled with tears, and she pressed a hand to her chest. "Ripley, I..." she had to swallow, her voice faltering. "I don't know what to say."

"Say that you'll let me honor you this way. I couldn't have got through this night without you or Henry. I could have birthed her in the snow and who knows…" She trailed off, closing her mind off to that thought track. Her gaze remained steady even as she began to cry. "You stayed by my side when I was terrified. You opened your home to a stranger. You showed God's true grace tonight. Please, Sadie. It seems only right."

"I did what anyone in our community would have done," Sadie owed her head, swiping at the tears that rolled down her cheeks. "The glory belongs to *Gott*."

Ripley smiled down at the little girl who now slept in her arms. Baby Sadie. The pain, all the moments of doubt, all the tears of the last five years, had led her to this moment. "It does, indeed. And for the first time in the longest time, I feel my faith once again. Not just because of this little miracle," her eyes raised to meet Sadie's, "but because of the kindness that you and Henry showed us."

"Then I accept," Sadie smiled. "*Gott* be praised."

"I used to think I had to do everything alone," Ripley said quietly, dividing a look around the room at those who'd stood with her tonight. "I grew up learning to rely only on myself. Last night has shown me that that isn't the case."

Nate touched his head to hers. "You'll always have me, honey."

"And you'll always have a friend here," Sadie agreed.

"Amen to that," Rachel pressed her hands together. "Right, let's get this little one fed. Then you must rest, *mamm.*"

Mamm.

Mom.

She was someone's mom.

She whispered a silent prayer of thanks, not just for bringing her daughter safely into this world, but for her journey so far.

"Welcome to the world, Sadie," she whispered. "I'm your mom. It's nice to finally meet you."

SADIE

*L*ast year had been Sadie's first Christmas and New Year as a Weaver. It had been busy, filled with laughter and chaos as the large Weaver family congregated in their home.

For months, the idea of being surrounded by Henry's boisterous siblings this year had been a source of apprehension. After all, she would have had to put on a brave face and smile her way through, pretending that everything was fine in her world so as not to worry them.

But the heavy snowfall had meant that they'd all decided to stay at home. It also meant that a local garage had been unable to get out to Nate's car, and it was still buried under a blanket of snow somewhere beyond the kitchen window.

Their *Englischer* guests didn't seem to mind the extended stay here all that much. The storm had put paid to any further travel until after the holiday.

Outside, the sun peeked from behind the gray clouds, burnishing the frozen lands. The storm had passed, and life would go on.

Sadie was also sure that her life would never be the same. Her namesake was a joy to behold. Fine dark curls and the sweetest face Sadie had ever seen. She didn't mind being woken in the dead of the night by her fretful cries. She paused, her gaze on the golden rays that forked the sky and let the warmth of happiness flow through her.

This Christmas day had many blessings: a new and unexpected friendship, a newborn to cherish and a beautiful winter's day to behold. And something else. Peace. A smile crossed her face, and she closed her eyes.

"Thank you for showing me," she whispered softly.

The sound of the back door opening drew her from her prayer. Henry stamped off his boots and hung his hat on the peg. He shook the water droplets from his coat and held his hand out for Nate's coat.

"Something smells delicious," Nate exclaimed.

"You wait 'til you try Sadie's fried chicken," Henry told him. He dropped a kiss on her head on his way to wash up. "Just like the cocoa, you won't find anything better."

Nate scented the air, his eyes gliding over the feast-laden kitchen table. A mound of creamy mashed potatoes and buttered vegetables. Golden biscuits and gravy. A glistening fresh apple pie. Peanut butter cups. Meat loaf and a fruitcake. Church windows and long John rolls. "Keep up the good care of us and we won't want to leave!"

Sadie laughed. "You are welcome to stay as long as you wish."

"I'm sure the sound of baby Sadie announcing to the whole community at three a.m. that she needs feeding will get real old real fast," he said with a laugh. "Where's Rip?"

"Upstairs resting," Sadie gestured to the roof. "I told her I'd keep an ear out for baby Sadie and wake her up if needed."

Nate gave her a pained look. "That's very

nice of you. Are you sure we're not in the way though?"

"You were outside helping Henry with the animals," Sadie smiled. "Besides, it's what we do in our community with a new mother. We all pitch in to lend a hand. It's a hard job. Which reminds me, Hannah Fisher dropped this off for you."

Nate took the beautifully wrapped parcel that Sadie handed him. It was dwarfed in his big hands. "Hannah who?"

"Our *nochber*."

"Your neighbor gifted us something? We've already been given that beautiful basket for Sadie to sleep in, and two blankets for her."

"Of course," Sadie shrugged. "A *boppli* is a wonderful blessing to be celebrated by all."

Nate seemed a little dazed. "That...that's so kind of her," his green eyes moved between them. "I'd better go check on Rip," he wandered from the room, parcel in hand.

"Tell her lunch will be ready in five minutes if she's hungry," Sadie called out as left.

Henry chuckled. "He seems a little overwhelmed by it all."

"Who wouldn't be?" Sadie turned to the stove and checked on the chicken drumsticks.

They were roasted to a perfect gold color, so she set them on a platter. "A new baby and gifts from people he's never even met!"

"Can you believe he's never fed a horse before?" Henry's eyes sparkled with mirth. "Someone of his stature would be a welcome addition to our community. We need some brawn around here come summertime."

"They live a very different life to us, but perhaps they will come visit when the fields are full of wheat," Sadie nudged some of the dishes on the table out of the way to make room for the drumsticks, then stepped back to survey it all. "Do you think this is enough food?"

Henry wrapped his arms around her from behind and nuzzled her neck. "More than enough, my love," he said between kisses. "There's enough food to feed us all for a week!"

Sadie delighted in his embrace, then patted his forearm. "Enough, Henry, what if our guests walk in? You wouldn't want to make them feel uncomfortable."

"Then all they would see is a man hugging his *fraa* and they'd know how much he loves her," he exclaimed, and he turned her around to face him so that he could frame her face with his hands. He studied her a moment, the laughter that lit his eyes fading into a more serious look. "How are you doing really? "You've been so gracious to our house guests, but I can't help wondering—are you feeling overwhelmed? If it's too much, I'm more than willing to take them to a motel."

She gave him a bright smile, letting her happiness shine through. "*Nee*, I am fine. Truly, I am. Ripley helped me realize something the other night."

Henry stroked her cheek, his eyes tracing her face lovingly. "What?"

"I've spent so much time focusing on what I don't have, that I forgot about the blessings I do have. A wonderful husband. A home to call my own. Food on the table. Our families. Our community. Good neighbors. A mother who made my childhood fun and full of joy. My health," she listed them all slowly. "New friends. *Gott* makes everything beautiful, and I forgot to look for the little things."

It still amazed her that they'd named their baby after her. She didn't think she'd done anything to deserve it, but she would cherish the gesture for the rest of her life. A smile crossed her face as she felt genuine happiness for Ripley. For the first time in a long while, she knew everything was going to be alright.

"I have so much to be thankful for, Henry. Ripley and Nate have been through so much more than us. I have hope in my heart, of course, but if a child is not in *Gott's* plan for me, then I still have so much in my life."

Henry released a deep sigh of relief. "I can't tell you how happy I am to hear that. I love you, Sadie." He gently kissed her. "You are my blessing. I thank *Gott* for you every day."

"And I love you," She said, her heart brimming with emotion. "I don't believe that Nate and Ripley being here was an accident. And now I have baby Sadie to rejoice in."

She heard their house guests coming down the stairs, which gave them time to compose themselves, but not before they'd exchanged a warm smile.

Ripley gasped softly as she held the door for Nate to carry the little basket through behind her. Baby Sadie slept soundly in it. "Sadie, this is incredible!" Ripley exclaimed, eyes wide in wonder. "Honestly, you are amazing!"

Sadie blushed and shook off the compliment. "I thought we'd have Henry's family here, so there is a lot."

Nate placed the basket on the countertop, the concerned father peeking into check on her before he grinned at the room. "I still can't believe she's here with us."

"*Believe* it," Ripley intoned drolly.

Henry slid into his seat at the table and the others followed suit. "Let us all pray and give thanks." They linked hands around the table and bowed their heads. His steady voice gave thanks for the meal and their new friends, and for the brand-new life in their midst.

Ripley squeezed Sadie's hand gently when he mentioned baby Sadie, and Sadie's lips curved in response.

"Amen," they each murmured as Henry finished.

"Here we go." Henry clapped his hands with glee, and they all burst out laughing.

The conversation quickly flowed as their plates were piled high with the delicious fayre. The tiny wails didn't do much to dampen spirits.

"I'll get her," Nate set down his fork and reached for his daughter.

"She might be hungry," Ripley said and held her hands out. Sadie watched as Ripley settled her daughter against her chest. "Did you see what Hannah gave us? Isn't it gorgeous?" The quilt was a patchwork of pinks and yellows, sunny and bright, like the dawn of a new day. "I shall have to thank her in person before we leave," she said.

"Here," Sadie took the quilt and covered Ripley so that she could nurse her daughter discreetly.

"Thanks. I feel like I need a dozen extra pair of hands with everything I need to do."

"It will get easier, I'm sure," Sadie returned to her seat.

"Okay, don't judge me," Nate announced to the room, and he picked up the bowl of potatoes. "I'm going in for seconds. And Henry, you were right. This is the best fried chicken I've ever tasted. Sadie, you're a genius."

Henry waggled his fork at Nate. "I told you. Now, Nate, tell me more about your work. Have you ever thought about setting up your own company?"

"I've suggested this to him," Ripley said to Henry, snagging a cookie. "Nate, you're too good for that company. Maybe you'll listen to Henry instead."

Sadie sat back, the contented smile flickering about her mouth, letting the conversation and gladness wash over her. Henry's face earnest as he spoke with a rosy-cheeked Nate. Ripley's face shining with the good-natured teasing she shared with her husband. The wriggling movements of a suckling infant under the blanket. A full belly and the sounds of laughter that lingered long after the moment had passed. This, she thought, was what the season was all about.

The kitchen windows had fogged with steam from the warmth of the kitchen. Beyond the glass, she could see the tiny flecks of snow tumbling from the sky once again.

They were all inside. Warm and safe. Full bellies, full hearts.

This Christmas day hadn't gone exactly as she had planned. It had been so much more. Sadie looked around the joyful faces gathered in her kitchen and knew that she was blessed in more ways than one.

Love and hope, mingling with the holy stillness that only Christmas can bring.

EPILOGUE

 ne year later...

SADIE LEANED FORWARD, standing on her tiptoes and pressing her forehead against the glass so that she could see further along the main road.

Nothing.

Not even a buggy passing by.

With a sigh, she turned from the window, wiping her hands on her apron as she surveyed the kitchen. It was a mess, sure, but every surface was filled with her tireless efforts from the past few days.

Cinnamon, roasted meats and baked fruit

pies mingled in the air. On the table, the turkey and ham joints took center stage. Cherry and pumpkin pies – Nate's favorite – alongside the chicken casserole and cornbread stuffing. A feast, for sure and certain.

Henry, sitting at the table, didn't look up from his bible. "You've heard of the saying a watched pot never boils, right?"

"Don't you have chores to do, Henry Weaver? Instead of being in here underfoot?" She asked, folding her arms across her dusty apron.

Her husband calmly flicked the page over, his eyes crinkling in the corners with quiet amusement. "I promised Nate I'd wait on chores until he got here so that he could help." His eyes slid to meet hers. "They'll get here when they get here."

"I can't help it," she looked through the window again. Snow dusted the yard. Not as deep as it had been last year. The roads were clear, the sky a pale azure blue. "It's been ages since we saw them."

So much had changed since the two strangers had happened on their doorstep, seeking shelter from the storm. Now, it felt as though Nate and Ripley were more *familye* than friends.

"Two months isn't that long," he pointed out. "They were here for harvest. And before that, it was summer."

Ripley had visited on her own in the summer. She'd spent almost a week with them both, and Sadie had loved every second of it. Nate's new business meant that he'd had to stay behind and work though they'd stayed in touch via a video call app that Ripley had shown them.

Sadie had spent the warm summer days baking cookies and teaching Ripley to sew, talking long into the evening whilst they sat out on the deck, baby Sadie sleeping between them, watching the sun sink into the horizon.

Letters had flowed between the friends, talking about news from the community and Ripley's part-time job and, of course, updates on little Sadie's progress. It had been tacitly agreed without question that they would spend Christmas day with them again this year, then head to Cleveland for New Year.

"I wonder if there's any more news on Ripley's *mamm*, and how her treatment is going," Sadie murmured.

"Why don't you ask her yourself?" Henry slid a marker in the pages of the book and snapped the cover shut. "That's a car I can hear."

HER HEAD SNAPPED to the window just as the car was turning into the driveway. "Thank goodness for your bat-like hearing," she clapped her hands excitedly and whipped her apron off. She darted out of the back door, the cold air slinking over her as she hurried across the covered porch.

The familiar silver sedan crunched to a slow stop in the middle of the yard. Her breath curled into puffs as she waited. Joy leapt when Nate's head appeared over the roof. "*Hallicher Grischdaag!*" he called out proudly.

Ripley's door popped and she climbed out of the passenger side, rolling her eyes at Sadie. "Sorry, he's been practicing that the whole way here."

"*Ach*, it's so good to see you all!" Sadie stepped off the porch, arms wide to embrace her friend. "Top marks for effort, Nate," she laughed, hugging him afterwards.

Ripley bent into the back door and

retrieved a dark-haired little girl who was already scrambling to get to Sadie. "Yes, yes, I know you love Aunt Sadie. Here you go," she passed her daughter over as Henry and Nate were exchanging a greeting of friendly back slaps and a handshake at the rear of the car.

"*Ach du lieva*! Look how much she's grown! Hello, little Sadie," she kissed the satiny cheek. "Oh, you've changed since I last saw you."

"Oh, has she ever," Ripley grinned. "Getting a personality to match."

Sadie stretched her arm out to encompass Ripley once again. "It's so good to see you."

"Come, come," Henry had his hands full of their luggage and gestured towards the open back door. "Let's get in out of this cold."

The house felt warmer when they stepped back in it, and the chatter filled the kitchen once again. The men took the bags up the stairs and then disappeared outside, where Henry could enlist Nate's help once again.

"You've been busy, Sadie," Ripley's gaze travelled around the interior. Cedar boughs and greenery adorned the mantlepiece and the furniture, and the glow of candles flickered around the room. "It looks beautiful."

"*Danke*," Sadie hung their coats up. "I

wanted to make it special for us all. *Ach*, it's so good to have you here. Please, tell me what's been going on with you."

They sat in the kitchen, with Ripley picking at the plates as they talked. Nate's new accountancy business was flying, and his books were full already, just as Ripley knew they would be. She'd returned to work part-time to at least have some money coming in whilst Nate was still finding his feet. Ripley felt torn about leaving Sadie though knew it was for their long-term plans.

The men returned. They stamped off the snow and joined them.

"Sadie, you've done it again," Nate rubbed his flat stomach, then said to Ripley, "Did you tell Sadie about how much of a hit you were at work when you took in the cookies for your work colleagues?"

Sadie's eyes moved to her. "You baked?"

"I did," Ripley grinned. "I followed the recipe you taught me in the summer. They all think I'm this baking genius now, though I'm kind of a one-trick pony. Those cookies are it."

"I can show you more," Sadie said quickly. "And your mom?"

"In remission for now," Ripley said. "Taking

it one day at a time. I'm meeting my brothers at her place for New Year."

Sadie nodded encouragingly. "That's good news. I've been praying for her."

"Me, too," Ripley replied with a quiet glance at Nate.

After the meal, Nate walked in bearing gifts. Henry unwrapped his – a thick, knitted jumper.

"Perfect for chilly starts in the barn," Nate told him.

"It's *wunderbaar*," Henry thanked him.

Ripley handed Sadie a small, flat package. Sadie gasped when she opened it and held it up to show Henry. Inside the simple, bare wooden frame was a pencil drawing of baby Sadie grinning. Sadie's breath caught as she studied it. "It's so thoughtful. Thank you both. We have something for you," she took the package out of a cupboard and gave it to Ripley.

She gasped when a stunning cream and blue quilted bedspread tumbled out.

"It's beautiful," Ripley ran her hands over the material. "It must have taken you hours."

"Now you will always have a piece of us in your home."

The sun dipped lower. They moved into the

siting room, where Henry stoked the fire to a healthy blaze. Sadie sat on a rug in the middle of the floor, watching her father with perplexity as he showed her how to carefully stack the colorful wooden blocks that Henry had made for her. She took one and tested it out with her mouth instead.

Sadie felt it – that deep sense of peace when everything was as it should be.

Henry cleared his throat, drawing Sadie's attention. He gave her a subtle nod.

Ripley, sitting on the other end of the sofa, sat up, her eyes narrowing with curiosity. "What was that look for?"

Nate looked back at her. "What look?"

Ripley moved her cup of cider back and forth between Henry and Sadie. "The Weavers. My spidey senses are tingling," she tapped the side of her nose. "Something is up."

Sadie laughed then. "I don't know what this 'spidey-sense' is, though, knowing you, it is movie-related."

"Correct," Ripley rolled her hands through the air. Her dark eyes regarded Sadie thought-fully for a moment, before they dropped to where Sadie's hands spanned the slight swelling in her abdomen.

Her smile was shyly radiant. *"Jah*, we're expecting."

The room erupted, scaring baby Sadie into tears. Nate dealt with his daughter as Ripley went to Sadie. She hugged her tightly. "Oh, Sadie, I'm so very happy for you. Oh, this is just amazing news. Tell me, when are you due?"

Sadie's cheeks were flushed as she parried the quick-fire questions of her friend. A year ago, she'd been uncertain and angry. But this woman had been brought into her life and had given her hope.

Her eyes drifted to Henry where he was making a funny face at baby Sadie. Then to the little girl in Nate's arms as he jigged her in a dance to make her laugh.

Her heart was full. Her faith restored.

WISHING MY READERS a Merry Christmas - Frehlicher Grischtdaag!

~ NAOMI ZOOK

The Renno Sisters - Tabitha

A woman with everything to lose. A man with a hidden past.

Tabitha Renno has struggled to maintain her family's farm ever since the tragic accident that claimed her parents. But when she discovers a secret that her father kept, her world is yet again tipped on its axis.

Before she has a chance to recover, Isaac Bowman, the source of everything wrong in her world, inserts himself into her life.

Isaac has never met anyone quite like Tabitha Renno. She is a far cry from his idea of an Amish woman. She is feisty and cantankerous. And he can't get her out of his mind.

Just when he believes he has made a big mistake in visiting the Renno farm, he is forced to spend time there.

Trapped, he begins to confront his painful past.

The Plain Road Home

Some secrets are too big to stay buried forever.

Caleb's mother fled the Amish community after his

father died, though Caleb had never forgotten his roots. He returns to a community that treats him with suspicion & nothing is quite as he remembers.

Lydia Raber remembers the day that Caleb Stoll left. She also remembers the mess that was left behind. There was a time she knew everything about him, yet the man who stood before her had been changed by the world he grew up in.

Caleb hears the whispers about his family's past. A family that was broken by secrets.

And when Caleb uncovers the heartbreaking truth, he questions everything he's ever believed in.

The plain road home is anything but smooth.

Who will be standing with him when the dust settles?

Fields of Faith

A collection of 15 uplifting, wholesome stories rooted in the Amish faith.

Join the various characters on their journeys through life's challenges as they seek love and strength within their community and beliefs.

All books are just 99 cents & available on Kindle Unlimited

ABOUT THE AUTHOR

Naomi Zook combines her love of romance stories with the Amish faith, having grown up on the periphery of it.

If you would like to be amongst the first to hear when she releases a new book and free books by similar authors, you can join her mailing list <u>HERE</u>

As a thank you, you will receive a FREE copy of her eBook

<u>The Wayward Amish Daughter</u>

Your details won't be passed along to anyone else and you can unsubscribe at any time.

Follow Naomi on <u>Amazon</u> for more details about her sweet Amish stories centered around faith & love.

Made in the USA
Middletown, DE
17 January 2025

69679699R00071